D1647676

SURFACE TENSION

A Collection of Flash Fiction

ALAN B. ZEMEL

Printed in the United States of America

First Printing, 2022

Print ISBN: 978-1-66787-331-2
eBook ISBN: 978-1-66787-332-9

Dedication

This book is dedicated to my parents, Laura and Sandy Zemel, for their steadfast enjoyment of my stories, especially in the early years when they weren't very good; their encouragement watered seeds and laid the groundwork for my career as a writer. In addition, to my best friend and writing coach Charles Bruce Aufhammer whose amazing insight as a writing teacher and author allowed him to peel back the surface-gloss of the stories and examine the written truths in relation to the characters and their worlds; his amazing talent and ability to find the truth is a gift that many of his writing students over the decades have appreciated. And, of course, to my wife, Pam Bellet, whose own talents as a writer and her gentle perseverance helped me to find the rough areas in my rewrites where greater attention and polish were required; her love, careful eye, and accurate insights proved the key to sculpting these stories and fulfilling this lifelong dream.

Special Thanks

Special thanks to my dear friend and colleague Eliot Cruz who used his extraordinary artistic talent and visual expertise on the cover design for this collection. He gave me exactly the opposite of what I had asked for, and, of course, as usual, he was right.

About the Collection

In the passing moments of every life come points where critical decisions are made, or enlightened realizations are achieved. None of us know when these moments will come, and sometimes we don't know when they have passed. So amorphous and fluid are these critical points in time that they often remain unseen even when their impact radically alters the path of a life. *Surface Tension* is a collection of flash fiction that catches characters in these moments, or approaching the brink of them.

Table of Contents

SURFACE TENSION

Shine

‖‖

He arrived alone near the Fifth Avenue and Spring Street subway entrance with the shoeshine pushcart as he had done with his father six days a week for three years since the end of the great war. The sun was beginning its ascent, and he stared at the Manhattan skyline, his fingers wrapped tightly around the pushcart handles, the skin under his grip, even at ten years old, already stained with waxy splotches of browns and blacks. Beneath his feet the tunnels that converged and connected Queens and Brooklynn to Manhattan began their morning rumble, and the rising sun seemed to reach down and organize the yellow taxis into neat lines along the Spring Street curb. The brownstones along Fifth Avenue began to cast short shadows, and in the distance sprays of orange began to penetrate the alleys. He had watched this scene play out hundreds of times while his father set up the shoeshine pushcart so that together, the pair could make the living that fed their family of eight. The boy had always marveled at how the city seemed to unroll and unfold beneath the waking sun, as if it were a plant, succulent and green, opening like a flower to embrace the day.

But today the city awoke in a way he had not expected and had never before seen. Today it awoke with an ever-louder cacophony of bangs, like a machine, broken, sputtering, moving forward in resistant fits. He noticed how the car engines revved discordantly, each out of tune with the next, and the taxis moved with screeches of rubber, sounding their horns while people shouted. Near him he could hear a door unlocking, and in the distance the chain-iron sound of a fire escape dropping. Beneath his feet, in the gutter, a cat screamed.

He backed against the wall, pulling his cart with him, and watched the city grind itself to life while men in dark coats and black hats emerged from the brownstones and made their way to the subway, to the city. He recognized some of them, they were his customers. He wished one would stop and ask about his father, none did.

He stood, mouth open, dry, his head leveling downward to catch glimpses of their shoes. He wished his father were there to call to the men, "SHINE?... FIX THE UPPERS?...FLASH YOUR STEP?..." but the man had died the night before, and all that was left of him was the shoeshine pushcart.

The boy sank to the sidewalk, his back sliding down the bricks, his legs folding, and his arms wrapping tightly around them, chin resting on his knees. His gaze, now closer to the pavement, could catch the parade of shoes marching in cadence before him. He could see their flaws: torn leather, grey creases, a layer of dust, splotches of mud, frayed laces, loose stitching. He knew how to fix them all. In his mind he called out loudly, "REMOVE THE SCUFFS?... MIRROR THE SHINE?... BLACKEN YOUR LEATHER?....CAP THE FRAY?" After a time, his mind quieted to the steady cadence of the words "polish...polish...polish...polish" moving like a drum with the pulse in his head. By noon a small collection of coins had appeared on the top of his cart, put there by those who mistook him for a street urchin. At one point he dozed, then woke with the urge to urinate, but he ignored that until it became a dull ache whose pain gave him a strange comfort. By one o'clock he began to think of his family and conjured an image of his mother standing at the stove boiling yesterday's bones, and, upon seeing him, looking up to ask what money he'd made. Together, he and his father would have made seven dollars for the day, alone she might expect him to bring home three, but if he walked in the door with less, he knew she'd be angry. By two in the afternoon he stood and shook his legs, the dull ache in his bladder had turned into an undeniable urge. He pushed the cart down an alley and used it to block the view as he urinated against a building. Once done, he sat back in his position on the sidewalk and watched the cars move and pulse with the rhythm of the traffic lights.

At four o'clock Andras Baba, returning from his work in the city, sat down beside him on the sidewalk and said through his thick Hungarian accent, "dis da papa ill today?" The boy looked up at him and said, "dead." The Hungarian looked down, shook his head, "se füle, se farka," then he looked up and explained, "It has no ears, no tail." The boy shrugged. "Means…no sense does it make." Then he handed the boy three single dollar bills, patted him on the head, and said, walking away "tomorrow, again, I see you for shine."

The boy pocketed the money and began his journey home, pushing the shoeshine pushcart that was the sum total of his inheritance: two folding chairs, two wooden boxes, two short stools, two sets of brushes, two hand-carry trays of polish, and a single stack of rags that still carried the scent of his father.

Departing Paris

|||||||||||||||||||||||||||||||||||||||||||||||||||||||||||||||||||||||||||||||||||||||||||||||||

The night before our holiday residence on St. Cirq Lapopie in Paris burned down Michelle and I had our last dinner there, blanquette de veau, her favorite, with a dessert of sherbet and chocolate covered strawberries which we dipped in red wine. There was cheesecake, but we were both too full to eat it, though she took a spoonful, smiled at me, savored it, eyes closed, breathing through her nose, chewing slowly, reluctant to swallow. Then we went to the bedroom and made love in glorious fashion, with a sense of urgency and desire we'd not felt since our first few months together nearly three decades previous. Later, I put French tulips on our bed, then cleaned the kitchen, loaded the dishwasher, and then set fire to the house.

Though Michelle burned with the house that night she wasn't killed by the fire; I had taken care of that while she slept. After our lovemaking she fell asleep and I lay awake watching, waiting patiently for her REM sleep. When I could see her eyes dancing and darting beneath the paper-thin sheath of her eyelids, I injected her with a heavy sedative, and then followed that with a massive dose of pentobarbital, a paralytic that slows the lungs and heart in such a manner that life departs as cleanly as rain escapes clouds. I used the tube coming from her treatment port, so as not to wake her, and she died in peace, in a dream, painlessly. I remember watching the weight of her sink into the mattress as effortlessly as ice cream melts in a bowl.

Once, on the patio in winter, warming ourselves over the fire pit as we picked at warm shrimp, we discussed this as an option to end the potential brutality of her upcoming treatments. We never spoke of it again, but in my mind I imagined we had…discussing it often, over dinner at Le Ciel de Paris, or over breakfast crepes and coffee, or on a walk down the Coulée verte René-Dumont. I imagined our calm conversations, logical debates, discussions of risks and mitigations, banter about percentages and pain, pillow-talk whispers as real in my mind as our first conversation thirty years previous at the Square Lamartine Garden. There she had asked me, a stranger to her then, a fellow American, a fellow college student, if I could help her switch her phone to the European network. I knew nothing of cell phones, but I fumbled with the device as if I had, and she sat beside me and watched. We etched out a conversation as I worked, both of us awkward in the hot sun. Around us a gentle breeze rustled a field of French tulips, and I remember how they stood tall and proud, blooming large and red in their spring season.

Adrift

H e read the poem again, as he'd read it most nights, after a scotch, through blurred eyes, a cigar smoldering in the tray next to his recliner, its smoke rising in simple thick strands that curled through the air moving unseen through the cathedral ceiling of his family room. She'd been gone for a year, his daughter, run over in the street at 14 years old while trying to fetch their dog who had escaped through the cat door. He'd found the poem on the desk in her bedroom the night of the accident, scribbled on the back of one of her water-color paintings, the front image awash with melted reds and yellows, a landscape of sorts.

Sometimes when he read the poem it seemed finished, and other times it did not. Sometimes when he viewed the watercolor on the opposite side it seemed finished, and other times it did not. He'd flip from one side to the next, observing them both with a faint realization that each act of creation needed the other, that they completed each other. It was all he had left.

At dinner, the night she died she had told him that the continent of Australia was adrift, that it had moved three feet north since she was born, and that the moon had also moved two feet from the Earth. He had argued with her, joking that changes of such magnitude could not go unnoticed. She had asserted that the majority of reality goes unnoticed, and then she asked him if he was aware of the 37 trillion cells in his body that were busy with the work of keeping him alive. He remembered offering a shrug in response, and then she had told him that everything is in motion, moving from one location to the next, floating on a web of shifting and unending impermanence. She had talked like this since her mother had died, and he was never able to understand the engine that drove her thoughts; now, a year after her passing, alone in his family room, reading her poem, viewing her watercolor, he felt himself drifting closer.

Waters Edge

O n the dock, at waters edge, she lets slip her gown and kneels, naked, her legs folding beneath, and then she leans back and spreads her arms to the sky, holding them there, open, as if waiting an embrace. Then she folds them in, leans forward, and begins to pray. She maintains this pose for a time as the water catches orange from the setting sun and ripples gently with an evening breeze. Her shadow floats beside her, curved, rounded by the arch of her shoulders and the manner in which the weight of her head seems to pull her forward. With her eyes half-shuttered she catches her reflection in the water. She moves to greet it, first her outstretched arms, then her face, then the rest of her, slipping the surface splash-less, her retreat from me so gentle it leaves no trace, no sound.

From my studio at the base of the dock I try to capture her, in oil, on canvas, my daughter. I've worked the painting in small increments through the years since she was a child, since she invented her beautiful ritual when she was eight years old. I had asked her the meaning of the ritual, she told me it was her way of returning to the world that birthed her. She performed the ritual every evening, when possible, and my effort to catch her has been a slow progression of strokes and color. I've crafted the world around her, the dock, the lake, the shoreline; those things that change little through the passage of time. I've taken liberties with the sun and shadow, freezing them to dusk clouds that seem to float position-less in the horizon, catching last light and throwing it to softening hues of orange. As for her, my daughter, I've drawn her into the scene several times and then erased her, over and over again, unsure at which age to capture her and complete the painting. But now, as she stands in the distance, I notice the curve of her hips and the way they open out to form the roundness of her backside which tapers down to her thighs, and I realize my time with her has ended, and so in this form I decide to offer her to the landscape; intertwining her with the surroundings, making the very particles that define her join the particles defining everything around her.

The painting complete, I close my eyes, and imagine her journey from the dock into the water. My daughter skims the bottom, her toes touching down in regular rhythm, kicking dirt. She finds herself in a school of fish and she swims with them, their eyes flashing silver in the dying light. She watches as their gills work, flexing, pulling oxygen from the dark water. The fish move around her and she joins their school, she moves as they do, she darts, she glides, she moves up, settles down, drifts. After a time she glances surface-ward, to the boundary between worlds, shimmering translucent with the start of a new moon. She swims on, through the silky touch, pushing and pulling her world, curious to find the currents that will land her. And then she moves to a place I cannot follow, and I lose her, all of her, even the vision of her, on my dock, as a child, and as I settle my brush I realize she has returned to the world that birthed her, and through that passage I understand my work is done.

The Catch

I steer my gondola gently toward the low arch of the Fondamenta dei Cereri bridge, where a girl, alone, maybe a tourist, with dark hair, leans over, staring at me, the hem of her knee-length skirt lifting and lowering with the currents of a pre-dawn breeze. Having not yet started my day as a gondolier, I am dragging a line from a pole tied to my seat, hoping to catch an elusive fish in the awakening canals.

I see her from a distance, a silhouette in the dawn fog, her elbows leaning on the rail, head propped on open palms. She seems at first an apparition, a product of my mind, something I might have formed from the shadow-light of the coming day. But as I drift toward her, my oar steady, the water lapping at my hull, she reveals herself; her legs bent slightly, her stomach flat, and I can see the curve of her small breasts and the nape of her neck; her skin is pearl, like porcelain, and I imagine that if I touch her, if I traced the curve of her young face with my index finger, she'd feel smooth and fragile, as though she might crack. I drift to a stop before her, and, looking up, I can see the rise of her thighs rounding their way up to her torso. Her eyes are half-closed but staring at me and for a moment I feel as though she might drift to sleep and slide gently into my boat.

"Are you alright?" I ask.

"Bored," she answers.

"Oh?"

"What's your name?" she asks.

"Gianni"

"Means God is Gracious."

"You speak Italian?"

"Scholastically. My parents have me in culinary school for the summer."

"Where?"

"Tuscookany…"

"Ahh…"

"I didn't know you were allowed to fish the canals."

"You need the proper permitting," I answer. "You can do anything in Venice with the proper permitting."

"What do you catch?"

"Very little," I say. "There are very few fish actually *in* the canals…they hide from us."

"Then why fish?"

"It's what I do," I say, "each morning with my coffee, I drift the canals for an hour, dragging a line before taking fares."

"Oh," she says, pulling in a deep breath, the aroma of early morning pastries rising on the breeze.

"Why are you bored?"

"I'm lacking adventure."

"Are you alone?"

"I'm *never* alone."

"I mean, in Venice, are you alone in Venice?"

"I'm with my parents. I'm *always* with my parents."

She looks around at the wall of buildings to the left of the canal, then to the right where the water laps against a set of stairs that lead down to the water. Then she looks at me, and with the rising sun I see a smile on her face, a calm, serene, perfect smile that seems born for her.

"I'd like a ride."

"How old are you?"

"Old enough," she answers, adjusting her position on the bridge.

"Age, I mean your age?"

"16…well, halfway to that."

"Aren't you too young for Tuscookany?"

"My Dad's friend is a teacher there…it's just for the summer."

"A free internship then?"

"Yes," she says, and adds, "I'd like to fish the canals with you." She looks at my line. Smiles.

"Have you done it before?"

"Once or twice."

"Oh."

We stare at each other, my gondola shifting with the current, my arms working the paddle to steady my position.

There is a tug at my line. I lift my pole and dangle a fish in the air; it struggles, gills moving, breathless. "A bissato" I say, "very unusual in the canals."

"Will you throw it back, or will you have it?"

"I will throw it back."

"You should have it."

"I do not want it."

"I think you do!"

"I do not."

"I can cook it for you!"

I do not answer.

"Let me cook it for you," she says, "I do know how," and then she runs from the bridge, rounds the sidewalk, and picks her way down the steps to the canal edge where she waves me over, excited, calling my name as if she has known me for years.

I float, oar in hand, and then I row toward her; at my feet the bisatto struggles and I feel its dorsal fin catch the meat of my bent leg.

The Chicken Man

I was sitting on a tire stop in the parking lot when a guy wearing a rubber chicken suit comes skipping out of the Smalls County Savings and Loan grasping a green canvas money bag. I was perched between a brand new green 1972 Pontiac Firebird Trans Am Tribute and a cherry red 1953 Chevy C-10 truck whose paint was waxed and perfect and clean but for the layer of rust starting under the wheel wells where you couldn't see unless you crouched low, like me. I was puffing on the second half of a discarded Belair 100 Menthol Light, low tar, a rare find that smoked smooth. I was hungry for lunch and scanning the parking lot for the glitter of coins lit by the noon sun shining on black tar.

Then this idiot emerges from the Smalls County Savings and Loan wearing a rubber chicken suit and grasping a green canvas money bag. He reminds me of what I had imagined the chicken man to look like as described on Armed Forces Radio during the Vietnam War; back then I'd see the chicken man after taking some long tokes while crouching low in the deep green, in the mud, the humidity rising; with my eyes closed I could see him bounding free and fearless through the mangroves, all yellow and red, hooting and hollering, drawing enemy fire.

And then all of a sudden he is here, all real and alive and skipping toward me having robbed the Smalls County Savings and Loan. I was thinking what a dumbass this guy was for wearing a rubber chicken suit to a robbery.

Then he's standing next to me and working his way out of his suit. He wears sneakers, jeans, and a white T shirt beneath. Then he jumps up and runs through an intersection like a pass-carrier in possession of the ball, his left arm clamping down on the money bag held in his armpit, under his shirt. Moments later a crowd sees me and they stand on the sidewalk outside the bank, some distance away, pointing. I hold up the chicken suit, I dance behind it, I laugh, I jump, the loose latex alive in my grasp. Then the police come. They come with guns drawn and one yells, "show me your hands," so I do. Then he rolls me onto my stomach, cuffs my hands behind my back, lifts me to my feet, and loads me into the back of a patrol car. As he does this he asks, "Are you the chicken man?" and I say, "Sure, man, in this life I am whatever you need me to be."

One of a Kind

G rowing up, I'd wait until no one was looking, or we were alone, and then I'd punch my brother. Not in the face, but in the arm, or thigh, or sometimes in the side. Nothing hard, nothing violent, just enough to get his attention, to let him know that even though we were identical, I was the one in charge. He made it easy. He never fought back and he never screamed, which really pissed me off, and he never told our parents, which pissed me off even more. Sometimes I'd make as if to hit him and then stop short. I could usually get him to feign away, or flinch, which I liked. He never knew if the fist would land, or where. Sometimes he'd not move a muscle, he'd just stare at me with those perfect glass-blue eyes, my eyes. I hated that he looked like me. I hated even more when Mother would dress us the same, comb our hair the same, and then ask her friends to guess which of us was Bob, and which was Bill. It felt like a circus act. I wanted to be one of a kind.

When we were eleven we were tossing the football in the street in front of our house and Mr. Jerkens, the junk collector from Coles County came down the road and ran him over. I saw my brother disappear beneath the truck wheels, saw the vehicle jump with the impact, heard the cachunk-cachunk of metal in the flatbed, and then watched the old man speed away, apparently unaware of what he had done. My brother lay in the street, and I could tell by the twist and turn of him that he was gone. I didn't run to him, I didn't call for help, I just stood there tossing the football several inches in the air and catching it, waiting, as if he would suddenly jump up and run wide so I could throw him a pass, a hard one, a perfect spiral, a bullet, one that would hurt when it landed.

Mrs. Castrigano came running from her porch screaming in broken English and pulled me by the hand toward her house. Once inside she sat me at her kitchen table and called the police. She was hysterical, screaming, crying, unable to catch a breath. She gave her address and kept yelling "Fratello…Fratello…Fratello." I held the football, I remember the feel of it, the rough texture of it, and I remember how the stitching would cross my palms. The police came, my parents came, the ambulance came, everyone came. I don't think Mrs. Castrigano ever stopped crying and yelling "Fratello." For the longest time I thought "Fratello" meant please, and help, and sorry; later I found out that it meant brother.

Impacts

‖‖

I stand at the loft door of the barn from which my stepsister and I once threw bales of hay to the ground fifty feet below. A strong summer wind turns a rusty weathervane on the gabled roof above, and I hear a shingle lifting and lowering in the breeze in regular cadence, probably loose and ready to fall, held in place by its last nail. The structure of the barn is old, abandoned, and I can hear its trusses creak and groan as gravity pulls it slowly down. The fields I once helped my father till are now sheets of tall grass, dancing gently with the breeze, their brown seed-stalks ready to drop. Sixty acres out, at the field's edge where my stepsister and I used to play, I see the familiar canopy of oak trees moving restlessly.

I close my eyes, inhale, and memory gives me the taste of freshly turned soil, the acrid scent of fertilizer, the clean perfect fragrance of things born and growing in the sun and rain. And from behind me, though she's been dead for over five decades, I can hear the footfalls of my stepsister against the freshly painted ladder as she makes her last climb to the loft from which, only moments later, she will jump and land on the ground several feet from where I stood then. I recall how I looked up and saw her leap, watched her swim through the air, a calm wonder on her face, staring at me all the way down as if she expected me to catch her. She had landed with a dull thud, the same sound as the bales of hay we'd toss down in summer. With the impact she bounced, her arms flailing, legs rotating as if to take a final step. I recall how her belly, then eight months pregnant with my baby, seemed to flatten as she settled in the dust, dead.

My father came running from the house. He shook me, and then lifted me off the ground with a shove. When I landed I heard the crack of bone but felt nothing.

Now, the weathervane turning above me, I'm aware of a familiar restless energy starting from within my legs and crawling outwards, toward my skin, touching my muscles and feeding them with the urge to move, to run. It's a feeling that has found me almost nightly, for decades, dragging me from sleep, making me flex and turn, twist and roll, demanding my attention, demanding my dreams. But now, on the other side of the passage of my life, my kids raised, my wife gone, standing at the loft door, the feeling comes strong, unencumbered by sunlight, free from the night. And, amidst the sound of the rusty weathervane, the flapping of a shingle, and the groan of trusses, it has also, for the first time, found a voice; I listen for a while, and, looking down, I imagine someone will catch me if I fall.

The Conversation

He rocked, smoked, drank; rocked, smoke, drank; the cigar in his left hand twisted curls into the air while in his right the cubes in his scotch bumped busily, rhythmically, against each other and the glass tumbler. The sun was setting, reducing the four-story retirement home on the other side of the lake into a stretched shadow that rippled and moved with the breeze as it shuffled the surface-water. His rocking chair squeaked on the way back, and groaned on the way forward. It was old, reaching four generations back to his great, great, great grandfather; the chair had long been the favorite of the family patriarchs, and now it was his. He used it often, almost always to welcome the ending of another day.

Two years prior he had stripped the chair of paint and stain, removing coated-layers that seemed to mark the passage of time like the rings inside a tree. He took the chair to the raw wood, oak. Once clean he had planned to apply a pickle finish and gift it to his son, Bob. At 38 Bob was buying his first new house and he and his husband, Joseph, had loved natural oak with a pickled finish; they had done their new house with it, all the cabinets, the kitchen, bathrooms, doors, door jambs, base boards and crown molding. The chair was to travel down another generation, but then Bob and Joseph were killed in an automobile accident, and there seemed no point to finishing the chair. Truth be told he hated pickled finishes. In the end he left the chair raw, and he liked the notion that its basic structure was naked to the air, grain exposed, vulnerable to the elements. His failure to finish the chair had little to do with the death of his son, and more to do with his feeling that things, all things, should be allowed the dignity of returning to their source. He had lived his life this way, burying his pets in the ground, seeing to it that his wife and daughter were buried the same way, in shrouds, open to the elements of earth and allowed in their last act to offer sustenance to new life, affirming the fact that they rejoined the world in a noble fashion.

Bob had wanted him to move into the four story retirement home across the lake. There had been a sales pitch, glossy pictures, a discussion about free meals, and bridge, and bingo, and ballroom dancing. There were discussions about the amenities, skilled nursing if needed, and a three-room condo that had cords coming out of every wall that, if pulled, summoned help. In that scenario he'd need no lock on his door, no help to come mow the yard, or fix the pipes, or bring him food in the winter; no longer a need for his five bedroom house on the lake where he'd raised his family and buried them next to his pets. That day he had made Bob a deal, he told him that if he'd divorce Joseph and marry a woman he'd move into the retirement community. It hadn't been that he hadn't liked Joseph, or his son's homosexuality (though he'd never understood it); he simply wanted a grand kid, someone to play games with, or throw around in a pool, someone there to ensure the chair continued its journey through time.

To that offer, Bob, sitting in his own rocking chair had answered, "Dad, the days are getting shorter and only the lizards are breeding." He'd not known what to make of that statement when Bob had said it; it seemed important and strangely complete, and so he hadn't asked for clarification, he just continued to rock and welcome the silence, happy to end the discussion.

Now, sitting in his chair, alone, staring down another dusk, he thought he'd like to continue the discussion, to ask for clarification, to hope to understand how everything could end in such quiet, anticlimactic and certain finality. He rocked, smoked, drank, staring off at the growing lake-shadows while several lizards shuffled past his feet.

Surface Tension

||||||||||||||||||||||||||||||||||||||||||||||||||||||||||||||||||||||||||||||||||||

B ob sat alone on the porch swing. James sat in the wicker chair across from him, his body rocking nervously, the woven wood beneath him creaking under his weight. "Are you OK?" James asked.

Bob kept his eyes low to the floor and did not answer, did not move.

The evening air was thick with moisture from the rain that had, only moments before, swept the area with gusty winds. Both boys had been on the porch swing shoulder to shoulder laughing about Mr. Bigelow, the math teacher who, while solving a quadratic equation on the chalkboard earlier that day, inadvertently let go a loud fart. Mr. Bigelow hadn't acknowledged what had happened, which made it even funnier to the boys, he just kept solving for "x" as if farting was just another sound his chalk made. When the rain came they had been howling about the incident as Bob made fart noises with a hand against his armpit. The storm had been a fast-mover and it ended as mysteriously as it had started, leaving the boys drenched, water running off their wet clothes and dripping through the roof slats, puddling on the porch floor. It was at that point, a moment after the storm had passed, in the silence that remained, that James leaned in and gave Bob a hard kiss on the mouth, with lips open and tongues touching. Bob had not pulled away, but James, suddenly shocked by what he had done, launched from the swing and fell into the wicker chair afraid he had just given something he could not take back.

"Are you OK?" James asked.

Bob sat, silent, looking down at the puddle on the porch, its surface broken only by the soft ripples made by a passing summer breeze.

James had been thinking about what would be his first kiss for many weeks, but in his fantasy he was going to give it to Jill, his neighbor who, through the years, he watched grow from a skinny-boned girl to fleshy young female. He had been planning the kiss for weeks, reviewing it in his mind, running scenarios, trying to figure out the logistics of the act such as how to approach it, when to do it, how long to hold it, when to pull away, where to look, and what to say when it was over. The more fantasies he had about the kiss the more anxious he became until finally, the only way to calm his nerves was to avoid her completely.

But just now, in the dark of the night, wet and fresh with fun, the kiss was given; it happened as smoothly as when they cast their lines into the water when fishing, and as innocently as when they dropped their trousers to jump naked into the lake.

"I'm sorry I did that" James said.

Still staring at the puddle Bob said, "Me too ..."

"Did you like it?"

"Yes."

"I've never kissed anyone before."

"I have, but never a guy."

"Then it's OK?"

"No, it's not."

"Why?"

"Because it means you're gay," and then he stood and swept away the porch puddle with the instep of his shoe.

Dinner

|||||||||||||||||||||||||||||||||||||||||||||||||||||||||||||||||||||||||||||||||||||||||||||||||

She, at the bar, flirting with the young bartender, asking his nationality and he, grinning, answers in broken-English then leans in, lifts her glass, and towels away the condensation beneath. Her husband, sitting beside her, picks at the cork of his coaster, a fine pile of shavings building on the bar. Then later, with the waiter, she is not pleased with the consistency of her lobster bisque. The waiter looks on, attentive, sympathetic, then offers another dish while her husband runs fingernails along the seams of his seat. Then, dinner re-delivered, she starts with the small talk; something about Frank, her boss, and the theme of the upcoming company annual gala, and then a mention of Sam, her co-worker, but not too much about Sam, just a mention, the tickle of a thought. He smiles, sips his wine. Then the maître d' comes to talk about the bisque, the consistency of the soup, the amount of the discount. He has large hands, meaty, and he places one on her shoulder and leans in close to make a soft apology while looking down at her plate, at her dress, at the way she wears her breasts. Her husband leans forward now, and she brushes the maître d's hand away. He bows, apologizes, leaves. Then there is talk about the grandkids, about having them every weekend until Thanksgiving, and plans to set a table for Christmas. Then there is talk about Janine, her hair dresser who just last month fell in love with her thirty-year-old son's best friend and plans on leaving her husband for him. Then back to the topic of Christmas, and a modified plan to take the family on a cruise rather than set a table. He doesn't remember having eaten but when he looks down his food is gone and his stomach, now tight, burns.

In the car, on the way home, she admits to having done all the talking and recognizes that she has not given him much opportunity to join in. She apologizes for not having asked about his company golf game the day before, about the new partner in the firm, about the car he is wanting to buy. She says that Dr. Martin, their marriage counselor, will not be impressed with her behavior this night. He nods. She reaches for his hand, the one near the shifter between them, the one laying as would a glove carelessly tossed. She intertwines her fingers with his and asks him what he is thinking. She waits for a response. It takes some time, but she waits. Finally, he says, "I feel," then he pauses, she squeezes his hand, says "yes?" and he continues, "I feel like I spent the night watching better men dance with my wife."

Letters from Amsterdam

|||||||||||||||||||||||||||||||||||||||||||||||||||||||||||||||||||||||||||||||||||||||||||||||

My Grandmother was from Amsterdam, and from a young age she had written the most vivid events of her life onto five-by-eight index cards that were the color of blue in the Netherlands flag. She had left me the cards, over a thousand of them, in her will. I think she understood that I'd appreciate them. I don't know if she could have guessed that I'd be able to see the essence of her in the curve of her ink; the consonants large and bold, the vowels light and smooth, the words moving across the pulp as elegantly as rivers cross the earth.

When I was eight years old we sat on the front steps of her porch, on a cushion, and I asked her what she wrote on the cards. She told me that life is not a successive string of events, as most people think, but about a single moment in time. I asked her which moment. She laughed, hugged me, and said, "so many...so very many." I hadn't understood what she meant, but it was important enough that I remembered the conversation, every detail of it, the bright sun, the smell of fresh cut grass, the sound of someone building something in a garage, the rev of an engine on a distant street, the chirp of a bird, and a breeze that set dandelion milkweed to the air. At the end of that day I wrote the image onto a five-by-eight card she had given me.

That's what we did, my Grandmother and I, when I was ten. On Saturdays I'd run the six blocks from my house to hers when the weather was nice. We'd sit on her front porch, on a cushion she kept in the front closet for this purpose, our feet resting on the top of three concrete steps that led to the entrance of her house. We'd enjoy the day while listening for the calliope of the ice cream truck. We'd hear it, moving street-to-street, back and forth, far, then near, then far, then nearer, and we'd stare at each other, a look of mock surprise on our faces, waiting, anticipating. In her right hand she'd shuffle coins; pennies, nickels and dimes rattling in the curve of her palm. Almost always the man across the street, Laddie Hampton, would take to his lawn with his engineless push mower, moving back and forth, shirtless and in shorts, his legs straining, his muscles flexing as he struggled to create fresh cut rows of green that opened the air to the scent of his clippings. He'd wave at us on every pass, and he'd smile, and my Grandmother would smile back. He lived alone, Laddie Hampton. I didn't know why, but as a child it seemed natural that old people should live alone. My Grandmother lived alone.

One Saturday, when I was twelve, I ran to her house. It was late, the sound of the calliope was already weaving the streets. I jumped a fence and cut through three yards to beat the truck. I could hear it making passes, back and forth, clean rows, distant then close, the music far then near. I rounded the corner of her street and sprinted through the clippings of Laddie Hampton's yard. I burst through my Grandmother's front door, the screen slamming behind me. I found her sitting at her kitchen table, staring expressionless at a blue card on the table before her. She pulled me onto her lap and hugged me. I sat, catching breath, caught in the curve of her. I watched her hand, steady and delicate, pick up a pen, hover over the card, then sink down and begin laying down words in steady rhythm, sentences unrolling onto the card in even lines, her hand passing back and forth, dropping lower in successive measured increments as she cried softly, capturing the moment Laddie Hampton collapsed and died in his yard earlier that morning.

A Passing of Lines

Kelsey Chapman sat in the nursing home, in a chair, next to his Grandmother's bed, working on his creative writing assignment. The lines of his pencil were dull against the yellow of his legal pad, and his words were awash in the cycling light of a neon bulb that poorly lit the room.

Granny Chapman, in her bed, watched him struggle, watched him write a word, then scratch it out, then write another, until the page was lost beneath a field of graffiti and he'd start again.

"What have you got so far?" she asked.

"Just crap," he said.

"Write this down," she said. He looked up at her.

"Start a new page and write this down."

He flipped his legal pad to a new page and readied his pencil. "Before I die I want someone to know..."

He looked up at her, his pencil stalled on the page. "Don't talk about dying."

"Oh for Christ sakes," she said, "I'll be dead by month's end, deal with it..."

"Sorry,"

"Don't be," she said. "Don't you ever be sorry about anything, or anyone."

"Ok."

"Now" she began again, "Before I die I want someone to know…"

He wrote.

"…that I made love with a bartender from Seattle."

He stopped. He looked up at her, his mouth open, preparing a response.

"Oh shut the hell up," she said.

"I didn't say anything."

"You were going to, so just shut the hell up."

"Ok," he said. He reached over and put his hand on hers.

"Are you going to write?"

He put his hand back to the page.

"I'm not senile, for Christ sakes."

"I didn't think you were."

"Your Mom thinks so, she's thought so since puberty… now write."

He steadied his pencil.

"Before I die, I want someone to know that I made love with a bartender from Seattle…in a barn, in July, when it was warm, and I was 16, and the hay beneath me was soft and loose. And back then life was undiscovered country, and the world glowed as if lit by a young sun, and the scent of it hung in the air like fresh cut grass.

'And when we were done making love, we lay together, naked and tangled, and he rubbed my back as if it were the only thing in the universe that was real and precious. And then we slept. And when we awoke we moved to the next moment, and then the next, and onward, through the years. And as we got older we often forgot how young the world once was, but sometimes we'd remember, and when we did we'd make love again, and when that happened I remembered the feel of hay beneath me, and it was soft and loose."

She stopped, eyes closed, drifting.

"And?" he asked.

"That's all I've got for you..."

"That's it?"

"That's all you need," she said. She reached out and touched his hand. "You know what?" she asked.

"What," he said.

"When I'm gone, if it's possible to miss a thing, the thing I will miss is you."

He gave her a kiss on the cheek. She pulled him into a hug.

The Evaluation of Mrs. Stick

Mrs. Stick sits in her wheelchair reading from the folder just placed in her lap by Attorney Mann. He says, "I thought you should know, this competency evaluation will be before the honorable Judge S. Samuel Wright on the twenty-fifth of this month." I think Attorney Mann has been retained by Bob and Sarah, Mrs. Stick's quinquagenarian twins from her first marriage when she was sixteen. They want the house, they want us out. Mrs. Stick reads the report quietly, her glasses crooked, ready to fall from the perch at the tip of her nose, her head angled backward so she can see through the best part of her trifocals. I have a premonition of the show that is about to start. I grin, then smile, wide. No one notices. The round and oily Mr. Mann sits, his briefcase in his lap, tilted up against his belly. The house is warm, and Mr. Mann is perspiring through his tight-white dress shirt, dark patches rising on the fabric.

Mrs. Stick looks at Mr. Mann, "Says here Mrs. Stick can no longer care for herself or others." She is firm, her voice hard. She has always had a caged and coiled energy, animal in nature, panther-dark, and I see it rising. "Says here Mrs. Stick is no longer able to ambulate," then she pauses, looks at Mr. Mann and repeats, slowly, "am…bu…late." Then she reaches back, activates her wheelchair brakes, places her hands on the chair arms, leans back as if to sneeze, then pushes forward and with a single motion she is standing. Papers scatter to the floor, her glasses dangle loose from a chain around her neck. The beast is free, I think it will run, and I am smiling, but still, no one notices.

"Says Mrs. Stick can't walk," and then she walks the length of the room and back, her meatless legs lifting and lowering in regular cadence, her head angled down, eyes floor-bound, giving her the look of a heron ready to pick in the mud.

She walks to Mr. Mann, stands in front of him, spreads her legs, shimmies forward onto his knee and lowers herself down. "Probably says Mrs. Stick can't fuck anymore," then she starts to hump his leg. Mr. Mann hugs his briefcase.

"Says Mrs. Stick is unable to toilet," she says, lifting herself off Mr. Mann. She walks to the bathroom, pulls the door wide, removes her Depends, and, standing above the toilet, lets loose urine that lands everywhere. We both watch her. When she is done, she cleans herself and returns to her wheelchair.

"Says Mrs. Stick is of an irrational mind," she says. "Well, fuck you," she says to Mr. Mann and then she yells "Stand." Mr. Mann stares at her. "I said STAND," and he does. "Now get the fuck out of my house!" she shouts. Then she pivots her chair so she is facing me, her back to Mr. Mann as he hurriedly gathers his papers from the floor. She smiles at me, winks. I smile back. Then she wheels over to me, leans forward, kisses my forehead. I don't feel it, but I appreciated the sentiment. I say, "Not bad, Mrs. Stick" but my words come out in their usual single wobbly hum, unintelligible. She nods, and says, "Yes," then adds, "Sons of bitches they are, Mr. Stick," and with that I am thankful she can still understand me.

A Prayer in the House of the Lord

||||||||||||||||||||||||||||||||||||||||||||||||||||||||||||||||||||||||||||||||||||||||

I recall my first exchange with Sister Theresa. I was 12. It was Sunday. I was with my catechism class during a service and we were in our uniforms; khaki pants for the boys, plaid skirts for the girls. I think I'd have been happier had they let me wear pants. Father Mathew had been weaving his way in and out of the ritual of prayer and explanation and he invited us to our knees in supplication. He had said, "and now, we offer this prayer to the Lord...." then he had paused, waiting to complete his sentence until the machine-noise of kneelers unfolding and the rustle of books and pages settled into the type of silence usually found in the deepest parts of libraries. As the congregation melted to their knees I had meant to join them, my body had moved to the edge of my seat, but instead of dropping to my knees I stood, alone, me, the only one. Father Matthew stared at me, surprised, as if he had just found a dead mouse in his pantry. He pointed at me, motioned me down, but I continued to stand.

That's when I heard Sister Teresa coming for me, the terrifying squeak of her rubber soles pressing into the floor under the pressure of her determination to reach me. And then her hand was on my shoulder, and she was pushing down, and leaning, and pressing. I felt her hand in the small of my back, and a firm pull on my shoulder as if she meant to fold me neatly like a piece of paper. Yet I stood, solid, a pillar of steel. The other kids looked up at me. Father Mathew, in front of his cross, watched, his lips parted, struggling against the compulsion to complete his unfinished sentence. Then, unable to force me down, Sister Theresa grabbed my arm above the wrist and yanked me from the bench, into the aisle, then down toward the rectory offices while I stumbled and stepped to keep her pace.

In the office, she pulled free a chair and forced me into it. In the distance I could hear Father Mathew finishing his prayer, the tenor of his voice echoing deeply through the sanctuary hall. Sister Theresa stood over me, her hands on her hips, breathing heavily. I recall the seams of her habit stretching and contracting as she found her calm.

Then she asked me, "why do you refuse to pray in the house of the Lord?"

And I said, "I *do* pray in the house of the Lord."

And she said, "then why not today?"

And I said, "I suppose I didn't feel like I was *in* the house of the Lord."

"For heaven's sakes" she exclaimed, "where in the world do you think the house of the Lord *is*, child?"

Anchoring my hands to the seat beneath my thighs I said, "For me it is deep in the woods where I'm covered by the canopy of sun and blue sky, or at night when I'm held tight in the clutch of trees."

I expected to feel the hard grasp of her hand on my wrist, this time to pull me through the church and straight to my parents' house where she would throw me like a broken doll in need of repair. Instead, she just stared at me, a smooth look coming to her round pink face and, after several moments she whispered, "yes, I know exactly what you mean," and then she sank down next to me, held my hand, and together we sat in silence.

Bloodfish Koi

The Redfish of Pimlic Sound have pink scales that layer their thick backs and blend toward blood-colored gills and wide white mouths. They have always reminded me of large goldfish, and in the summer of '36, when I was twelve, my friend Jilly and I named them the Bloodfish Koi. We fished the Bloodfish Koi through the summer of '36, pulling them from the Sound day-after-day, week-after-week, month-after-month, for no other reasons than to see who could cast the farthest and smoothest line. We'd leave them to die on the rocks of the Pimlic Sound, and then at the end of the day we'd compare our catches like we use to compare marbles when we were ten.

The following summer of '37, we pulled hundreds from the Sound. We sold them at the market for fifteen cents each. We caught them with lines, with nets, and with our hands. We fished them through the fall, right into December when they should have migrated South to avoid the winter. But the Bloodfish Koi were not gone, and I began to realize that something was terribly wrong with the fall of '37; it was too warm for the month, and the Koi pressed on in huge numbers, darting and dancing in the Sound outside my bedroom window. The heat of the summer seemed stuck, trapped beneath layers of blue-belly clouds that hung low through the weeks, their shapes shifting, melting, and reforming in the currents of the atmosphere. The air was like thin worn silk, and when you walked outdoors it pooled on the surface of your clothes and worked its way to your skin, where it would settle, make you feel weak, and give you the fever-flu. From my window I could see it hanging there, waiting, as solid and real as the brown mud suspended in the waters of the Sound.

That year it killed twenty-five people, including Jilly, my Mother, Reverend Bob, and Doc Harper. It tried to kill me, but I refused to be caught. I stayed in my bedroom, took my meals there, and watched it hovering above the sound, above the Bloodfish Koi, like a dark smoke whose acrid scent I could taste seeping through the loose gaps around my window frame.

I had warned my Mom about it, but she said I was crazy. She tried to push me out of the house to go play, or chop wood, or help dad with the barn, but I refused to leave my room. Mom sent for Reverend Bob to see me. I warned him to lock himself in his church, and to take the hobos with him. I told him to stock food for the winter. One day Jilly came by, and I warned him, too. He said I was nuts. I told him we had killed too many Bloodfish Koi that year, and that God was angry, but he just laughed and told me that God had no limits on the number of Bloodfish Koi two thirteen-year-old boys could pull from the Pimlic Sound in a single year. He died a month later.

Now, twenty years later, I sit in my son's room, once my room, looking out of the window at the Sound, and another December run of Bloodfish Koi. Earlier that day my son, having just turned ten, wanted me to take him fishing, but I told him no. He had cried, and

I tried to make him understand the danger of fishing the Bloodfish Koi. Later that day I caught him pulling Koi from the river with two thirteen-year-old boys who lived two farms down. They had pulled a dozen from the Sound. They had caught them with lines, with nets, and with their hands. The Koi littered the banks of the Sound, and their stench hung in the air, spoiling in the unnatural heat of the December sun. Now, at this window, I think about the air being thick, like it was then, and humid. Earlier that day it had hung like a curtain beneath a layer of blue-belly clouds. I closed the window to lock it out.

That night I stood in the doorway for a moment and listened to the calm confident sound of my son's lungs pulling and pushing air. Then I left a note for my wife to keep our boy indoors until March. I took my fishing pole from my foyer closet where it had stood for twenty years. I left the house. I was in my bathrobe, my feet bare, the gravel of my driveway sharp on my feet, and the rocks of the Pimlic Sound cold, slippery. I shook my fishing pole, my line not baited, not even hooked. I cast my line with a firm throw, and though the line was only single-weighted it traveled a good distance and landed with a solid plunk. I dangled my feet in the water, and waited. I thought about Mom, about Reverend Bob, about Doc Harper, about Jilly. I imagined that I could see them in the evening fog that builds over the Sound, over the Bloodfish Koi. My eyes drifted closed, and I felt the warmth of the season on my face. I breathed the acrid taste of a December that is too moist, too perfect. And then my line tugged, and when that happened it dawned on me that God fishes people from our town as easily as two thirteen year old boys fish Bloodfish Koi from the Pimlic Sound. I allowed the line to pull me, from my rock, into the cold water, and I waded out with the pull of it, and as the water reached my chest I wondered how much God would get for me when he pulls me free and leaves me to spoil washed up on the rocks of the Pimlic Sound.

Family Trilogy

||||||||||||||||||||||||||||||||||||||||||||||||||||||||||||||||||||||||||||||||||||

Early Journal

He writes in his journal: "I want to win the heart of X." He is a video game designer, and most of what he does, including writing in his journal, is a fiction. The only thing he knows that is not a fiction is that he wants to win the heart of "X." He doesn't know who "X" is, and he doesn't care about her age, size, shape, religion or politics. He's not particular, he's not picky, he doesn't care; he's angry, and he's sad, and he's never won the heart of anyone.

On The Road

He drives, she sleeps. It is always like this when they travel long distances, and he does not like it. He wishes she'd wake up and look out the window, make a comment about the mountain passes, play with the radio, say she needs to pee, or eat, or stretch her legs. He is tired, and the road is tight; guard rails are sometimes there, sometimes not. He fantasizes about driving off the edge, about her waking up on the way down, in free-fall, and he wonders if she'd live long enough to regret not having kept him company.

Cufflinks

He, head down, twists his gold cufflinks while she watches and sips her near-empty glass of wine. They sit on the bench in their back yard; it is morning and they've been up all night, fighting. Their children play in the yard. The sun has risen and is direct and strong upon them. She perspires, he does not. He never perspires, not even during sex, and as she studies him she discovers this is why she hates him. His inability to show discomfort infuriates her.

"It's hot today," she says.

He looks up, "not particularly," he says.

He returns to his cufflinks, she to her wine.